NANCY DREW
girl detective

PAPERCUTZ™

NANCY DREW GRAPHIC NOVELS AVAILABLE FROM PAPERCUTZ

#1 "The Demon of River Heights"

#2 "Writ In Stone"

#3 "The Haunted Dollhouse"

#4 "The Girl Who Wasn't There"

#5 "The Fake Heir"

#6 "Mr. Cheeters Is Missing"

#7 "The Charmed Bracelet"

#8 "Global Warning"

#9 "Ghost In The Machinery"

#10 "The Disoriented Express"

#11 "Monkey Wrench Blues"

#12 "Dress Reversal"

#13 "Doggone Town"

#14 "Sleight of Dan"

#15 "Tiger Counter"

Coming February '09
#16 "What Goes Up..."

$7.95 each in paperback, $12.95 each in hardcover.
Please add $4.00 for postage and handling for the first book, add $1.00 for each additional book.

Please make check payable to NBM Publishing. Send to:
Papercutz, 40 Exchange Place, Suite 1308 New York, NY 10005, 1-800-886-1223
www.papercutz.com

#15

Tiger Counter

STEFAN PETRUCHA & SARAH KINNEY • Writers
SHO MURASE • Artist
with 3D CG elements and color by CARLOS JOSE GUZMAN
Based on the series by
CAROLYN KEENE

New York

Tiger Counter

STEFAN PETRUCHA & SARAH KINNEY – Writers
SHO MURASE – Artist
with 3D CG elements and color by CARLOS JOSE GUZMAN
BRYAN SENKA – Letterer
MIKHAELA REID and MASHEKA WOOD – Production
MICHAEL PETRANEK - Editorial Assistant
JIM SALICRUP
Editor-in-Chief

ISBN 10: 1-59707-118-8 paperback edition
ISBN 13: 978-1-59707-118-5 paperback edition
ISBN 10: 1-59707-119-6 hardcover edition
ISBN 13: 978-1-59707-119-2 hardcover edition

Printed in China.
Distributed by Macmillan.

10 9 8 7 6 5 4 3 2 1

NANCY DREW, HERE, WITH NO INTENTION OF WRESTLING THIS ALLIGATOR!

CLARICE

IN NATURE PRESERVES, ***SOME*** MISGUIDED HUMANS TRY TO FEED THEM, WHICH IS EXTREMELY DANGEROUS, ENCOURAGING ALLIGATORS TO APPROACH HUMANS AGGRESSIVELY, EXPECTING FOOD.

SOME PEOPLE THINK IT'S CRUEL TO SUPPRESS WHAT ARE SOME-TIMES DANGEROUS INSTINCTS.

OTHERS HAVE NO PROBLEM BUYING A BABY ALLIGATOR AT THEIR FRIENDLY EXOTIC PET SHOP AND RAISING THEM IN THEIR BATHTUBS, AS PETS.

THE PROBLEM WITH KEEPING WILD ANIMALS FOR PETS IS...

CHAPTER ONE: CAT NAPPING

...THEY DON'T ALWAYS BEHAVE LIKE PETS!
AHHH!
HSSSS
IT'S ALL RIGHT, NANCY. EVEN I STILL GET A LITTLE JITTERY AROUND THE CRITTERS WITH THAT MANY TEETH.
JACK KINGSLEY RAN THE RIVER HEIGHTS ANIMAL PROTECTION CENTER. HE'D SAVED JUST ABOUT EVERY IMAGINABLE KIND OF ABANDONED, LOST OR MISTREATED PET.
I'M USUALLY BUSY SOLVING MYSTERIES WITH MY BEST FRIENDS, GEORGE AND BESS.
BUT, MYSTERIES HAD BEEN IN SHORT SUPPLY, LATELY, SO WE ALL DECIDED TO GET IN TOUCH WITH OUR INNER ANIMAL LOVERS BY VOLUNTEERING.
RIVER HEIGHTS ANIMAL PROTECTION CENTER

JACK SAYS TAKING IN AN ANIMAL AS BIG AS THAT ALLIGATOR IS TOTALLY UNUSUAL! SO, WHAT ARE THESE BIG CAGES USED FOR?
SMELLS LIKE ELEPHANTS!
RIINNG RIINNG
TAKE A BREAK FROM THE SMELLY JOB, GIRLS!
I GOT A CALL! A LADY'S CAT'S BEING ATTACKED BY A COYOTE! LET'S RIDE!
A COYOTE?!
JACK HAD BEEN REALLY GOOD ABOUT LETTING US HELP IN EVERY ASPECT OF THE CENTER'S OPERATION.
BUT WE'D NEVER GONE ON A RESCUE CALL BEFORE. THIS WAS COOL.

WE DROVE DEEP INTO THE RIVER HEIGHTS WOODS TO THE COTTAGE OF MRS. EARTHA.
GIVEN HER LOCATION, IT WAS NO BIG SURPRISE SHE WAS HAVING CLOSE ENCOUNTERS WITH WILDLIFE.
BIG MONGREL CARRIED MY POOR TUNSIS INTO THE SHED! GET HIM!
IT'S A DOG EAT CAT WORLD AND SOMETIMES NATURE SEEMS CRUEL.

BUT, WHILE HUMANS ARE THE DEADLIEST CREATURE ON THE PLANET...

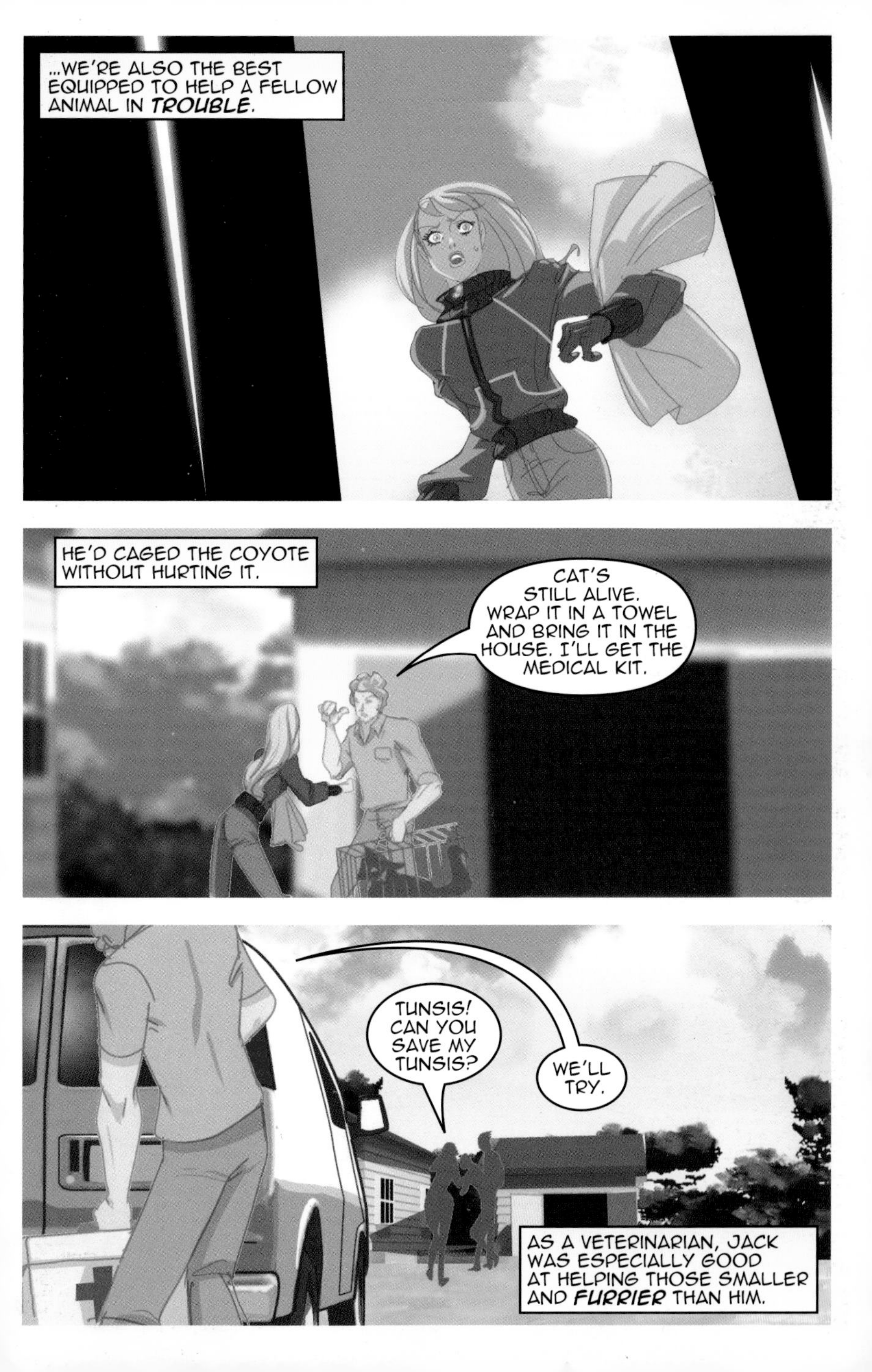
...WE'RE ALSO THE BEST EQUIPPED TO HELP A FELLOW ANIMAL IN TROUBLE.
HE'D CAGED THE COYOTE WITHOUT HURTING IT.
CAT'S STILL ALIVE. WRAP IT IN A TOWEL AND BRING IT IN THE HOUSE. I'LL GET THE MEDICAL KIT.
TUNSIS! CAN YOU SAVE MY TUNSIS?
WE'LL TRY.
AS A VETERINARIAN, JACK WAS ESPECIALLY GOOD AT HELPING THOSE SMALLER AND FURRIER THAN HIM.

SOME FEEL THAT WE DIDN'T DOMESTICATE CATS AS MUCH AS THEY DOMESTICATED US.
THE ANCIENT EGYPTIANS REVERED CATS, THINKING THEY HAD MAGICAL POWERS.
THERE ARE THOSE AMONG US WHO STILL SEEM EASILY HYPNOTIZED BY THE FURRY FELINES.
CLEARLY, MRS. EARTHA HAD FALLEN UNDER THE SPELL OF CATS!

NO WONDER THE COYOTE CAME SNIFFING... IT'S A REGULAR SMORGAS-BORD.
LOOKS LIKE WE HAVE A HEALTH VIOLATION HERE, MRS. EARTHA.
THE CITY HAS A LEGAL LIMIT OF THE NUMBER OF ANIMALS YOU CAN KEEP UNDER ONE ROOF.
JACK WAS ALL BUSINESS WHEN IT CAME TO PUBLIC HEALTH CODES.
WHA- WHAT ARE YOU GOING TO DO? GIVE ME A TICKET?! I'M ***BROKE***, LIVING ON A FIXED INCOME!

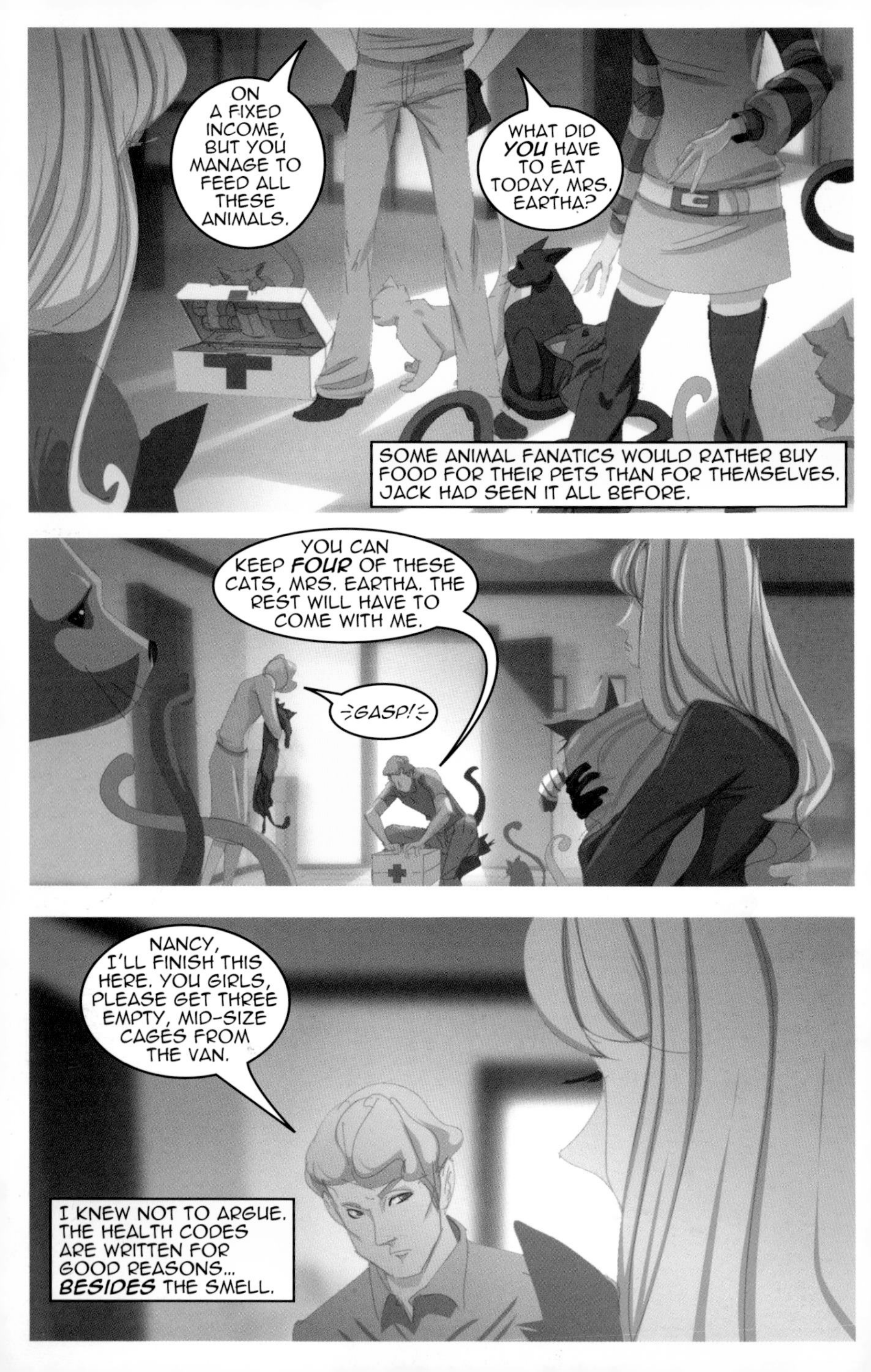
ON A FIXED INCOME, BUT YOU MANAGE TO FEED ALL THESE ANIMALS.
WHAT DID *YOU* HAVE TO EAT TODAY, MRS. EARTHA?
SOME ANIMAL FANATICS WOULD RATHER BUY FOOD FOR THEIR PETS THAN FOR THEMSELVES. JACK HAD SEEN IT ALL BEFORE.
YOU CAN KEEP *FOUR* OF THESE CATS, MRS. EARTHA. THE REST WILL HAVE TO COME WITH ME.
GASP!
NANCY, I'LL FINISH THIS HERE. YOU GIRLS, PLEASE GET THREE EMPTY, MID-SIZE CAGES FROM THE VAN.
I KNEW NOT TO ARGUE. THE HEALTH CODES ARE WRITTEN FOR GOOD REASONS... *BESIDES* THE SMELL.

I GUESS THIS IS THE SADDER SIDE OF ANIMAL RESCUE.
YEAH, KIND OF MAKES CLEANING CAGES SEEM FUN!
WE VOLUNTEERED TO HELP ANIMALS, REMEMBER.
CLEANING CAGES AND BREAKING OLD LADIES HEARTS... ALL JUST PART OF THE JOB.
I GUESS EVEN JACK'S FIRST SEIZURE MUST HAVE BEEN TOUGH. BUT, HE SEEMED HARDENED BY EXPERIENCE.
HMM. THERE ARE THOSE BIG CAGES AGAIN.

YOU DIRTY, NO-GOOD SO AND SO!
YOU CAN'T TAKE MY BABIES! I'LL GET YOU FOR THIS!
SORRY, MA'M! I HAVE TO DO MY JOB.
AND KEEP THE REMAINING FOUR CATS INSIDE!
COYOTES OFTEN TRAVEL WITH A MATE OR IN A SMALL PACK, SO THERE'S LIKELY MORE AROUND.
MORE?! GASP!

WHAT DID MR. SO AND SO SAY ABOUT MORE COYOTES?

MAYBE I SHOULD STOP AT HOME TO MAKE SURE MY TOGO IS INSIDE!

TOGO WAS A BRAVE LITTLE DOG WHO'D ADOPTED ME A WHILE BACK. I SUSPECTED HE WAS LIKELY TO TAKE ON A HUNGRY PACK OF COYOTES, BUT NOT LIKELY TO WIN!

BUT, SUDDENLY, MY DAY TOOK A WHOLE *DIFFERENT* DIRECTION.
HEY, THERE'S JACK'S VAN. THIS ISN'T THE ROAD BACK TO THE ANIMAL SHELTER.

HE MUST HAVE BEEN SCOUTING FOR MORE COYOTES...
...AND SEEN THIS *ACCIDENT*!
BETTER CHECK IT OUT.

IT CERTAINLY SEEMED LIKE JACK HAD STOPPED TO HELP. THE DRIVER LOOKED VERY SHOOK UP.

AND HE MUST HAVE CALLED THE POLICE.
BUT, WHY DID CHIEF McGINNIS ***HIMSELF*** COME OUT?
I WAS TRANSPORTING A ***TIGER*** TO A--A ***CIRCUS*** WHEN I MUST HAVE ***DOZED*** AND HIT A TREE. THEY RAN INTO THE WOODS.
THEY?

I... I MEAN ***IT!***

OKAY, PAL. I'M GOING TO CALL EMS TO LOOK AT YOU. YOU'RE LUCKY I HAPPENED TO BE CRUISING BY!
EMS? NO! I'M FINE. JUST SHOOK UP IS ALL.

HUH. SO, JACK *HADN'T* CALLED THE POLICE.

I'D BE SHOOK UP, TOO IF I'D JUST LOST MY TIGER! HUH? IN FACT I *AM* SHOOK UP, TOO!
THERE'S A TIGER LOOSE!

WHILE McGINNIS GOT THE STORY, I POKED AROUND.

THERE WERE BIG CAGES, LIKE THE ONES IN JACK'S TRUCK. THEY'D ALL FALLEN AND BROKEN IN THE CRASH.

I FINALLY ASKED....
HEY, JACK. WHAT ARE THE BIG CAGES FOR... THE ONES IN YOUR VAN AND IN THE SHELTER?

THAT'S A VERY TIMELY QUESTION, NANCY. THEY'RE FOR BIG CATS!
LIONS AND TIGERS THAT ARE NO LONGER SUITABLE FOR PETS.
PETS?!

I COULD BARELY STAND THE SMELL OF MRS. EARTHA'S **SMALL** CAT HOUSE. WHO'D WANT A LION OR A TIGER FOR A PET?
ANYONE WHO **LOVES** TO HUG AND SQUEEZE THE CUTE AND SOFT AND FURRY AND CUDDLY, BIG SMOOSHIE WOOSH!
WELL, I **GUESS** IT WOULD BE **EXCESSIVE** TO HAVE A SMOOSHI WOOSH **THAT** BIG.

ACTUALLY, THE NUMBER OF BIG CATS BEING SOLD AS PETS IS PRETTY STAGGERING.
MOST OF THEM ARE CAUGHT AND IMPORTED FROM ASIA. SOME ESTIMATE THERE ARE TEN TO FIFTEEN THOUSAND LARGE CATS IN THE HANDS OF PRIVATE OWNERS HERE IN THE UNITED STATES.
SOME STATES, LIKE OURS, HAVE LAWS BANNING PRIVATE OWNERSHIP OF BIG CATS, BUT IF YOU'RE WILLING TO PAY, YOU'LL FIND SOMEONE WILLING TO SELL YOU ONE.
BUT, THE COST OF FEEDING THEM AND THE DIFFICULTY OF CARE ARE NOTHING COMPARED TO THE DANGER... SO LOTS OF FOLKS EVENTUALLY ABANDON THEM TO THE RESCUE ORGANIZATIONS.
THERE'VE BEEN SO MANY, THE SHELTER IN THE NEXT TOWN HAD TO BUILD A SPECIAL HOLDING PEN FOR LIONS AND TIGERS!

YOU ARE JUST VOLUNTEERING AT THE SHELTER, RIGHT? I'M IMPRESSED BY HOW MUCH YOU KNOW!
NOT ME! I'D BE SURPRISED IF NANCY DREW HADN'T DONE ALL HER HOME-WORK!
THANKS, GUYS. BUT, MAY I TALK TO YOU IN PRIVATE A SECOND?
THE DRIVER IS PRETTY NERVOUS. IT'S POSSIBLE THIS GUY WAS TRYING TO SELL THE TIGER, ILLEGALLY.
HMM.
I DON'T KNOW... IT CERTAINLY IS POSSIBLE, BUT I THINK HE'S JUST SHAKEN FROM THE ACCIDENT.
EVEN SO, I'LL CHECK HIS PAPERS AND I.D. ...

SO, HOW'S ABOUT SHOWING ME THE PAPER-WORK ON THAT TIGER OF YOURS?
Y'KNOW, THERE'S A REALLY FUNNY STORY ABOUT THAT.
I WAS JUST LOOKING FOR THE PAPERWORK, BUT IT'S GONE!
MUST'VE BLOWN OUT THE BACK WHEN THE DOORS OPENED IN THE CRASH.
REALLY?! WELL, I'LL ALSO NEED TO SEE YOUR LICENSE AND REGISTRATION... ASSUMING YOU KEEP THOSE SOMEWHERE SAFER?
YES, SIR! RIGHT HERE IN THE GLOVE COMPARTMENT, OFFICER.

GEE, AND HERE I WAS WORRIED ABOUT THE COYOTES.

YEAH. NOW, THE COYOTES HAVE SOMETHING TO WORRY ABOUT.

THAT TIGER'S PROBABLY SCARED AND DISORIENTED. WITH ANY LUCK IT'LL STAY IN THE WOODS UNTIL WE FIND IT...
...AND WON'T HEAD FOR TOWN.

GIRLS...
YEEIAAH!
SORRY. DIDN'T MEAN TO STARTLE YOU.
BUT, I THINK I'D BETTER GO AFTER IT BEFORE IT GETS TOO FAR.
Y-YOU'RE GOING TO SHOOT IT?!
TRAN-QUILIZER GUN. PUTS IT TO SLEEP. I'LL WAIT HERE UNTIL YOU GIRLS GET SAFELY BACK IN YOUR CAR.
THEN I'LL SEARCH THE WOODS.

YES, GIRLS! TIME FOR YOU TO GET **HOME** WHERE IT'S **SAFE**.
RIGHT?
BUT, I FOUND THE **TRACKS**. LOOK!
THEY'RE TIGER TRACKS, ALL RIGHT!
NANCY DREW, DON'T EVEN **THINK** ABOUT IT!
YOU MAY BE A MASTER SLEUTH, BUT **PLEASE** LEAVE TRACKING MAN-EATING ANIMALS TO THE **PROS**.

CHIEF McGINNIS KNOWS BETTER THAN TO CHALLENGE ME THAT WAY. HE MUST BE OFF HIS GAME TODAY.
MAYBE. BUT, HE'S RIGHT. I ONLY HAVE ONE OF THESE. SO, LEAVE THE HUNTING TO ME.
HERE'S MY LICENSE AND REGISTRATION FOR THE VAN.
HMPH!
NOW GET BACK IN THE TRUCK AND WAIT FOR THE MEDICS, WHILE I RUN A CHECK ON THESE.
UM. YESSIR!

HI, CHIEF!
HELLO, GEORGE! CAN I HELP YOU? I'M A LITTLE BUSY HERE.

WOW, IS THAT YOUR NEW MOBILE DATA TERMINAL? AWESOME!

YEP. ISN'T THIS BABY SOMETHING? I USED TO HAVE TO CALL IN AND GET A SERGEANT TO GET THE INFO ON *HER* COMPUTER AT THE STATION.
NOW, THE MDT PUTS IT ALL AT MY FINGERTIPS.

COOL! LEMME SEE!
COOL AND **CONFIDENTIAL**, YOUNG LADY. NOW, SLOWLY BACK AWAY FROM THE VEHICLE.
HELLO! DANG IT! THIS FELLA'S LICENSE HAS BEEN SUSPENDED!
HE'S DRIVING ILLEGALLY AND--

VRRRMMM
HUH?!
WHAT THE HECK IS HE DOING?!
CLUNK

YEIIIKES!
CLUNK
VROOOMMMM
CLUNK

OOOMPH!

HUH?! HE LEFT WITHOUT HIS TIGER!

CLEARLY, NEITHER HE ***NOR*** THE TIGER HAS ANY INTEREST IN BEING ***CAGED***.
END CHAPTER ONE

UNFORTUNATELY, A HIGH-SPEED CHASE WASN'T POSSIBLE WHILE CHIEF McGINNIS HAD A CIVILIAN PASSENGER WHO'D, UH, *DROPPED IN*.
HE'S GETTING AWAY!
OUT OF THE CAR, GEORGE! *NOW!*
CHAPTER TWO: TIGER WOODS

RIGHT! YES, SIR! GETTING OUT NOW!
VRRROOOM

DON'T WORRY! YOU'LL GET HIM, CHIEF!

SORRY ABOUT BREAKING YOUR NEW MDT!

HIS BRAND NEW MDT?! YOU BROKE IT?!
THIS IS SUCH A BAD DAY! HE PROBABLY HATES ME NOW, HUH?!

GIRL, YOU'D BETTER NOT SO MUCH AS JAYWALK!

OH, GEORGE. HE'LL FORGIVE YOU.
YEAH, BUT HE PROBABLY WON'T FORGET ANY TIME SOON!

FORGET IT. I'M SURE IT'S INSURED. LET'S GO!

GO WHERE? YOU HEARD THE CHIEF! HE TOLD US TO STAY PUT!
HAH! AS IF *THAT* EVER STOPPED HER.
HEY, I LET THE CHIEF CALL THE SHOTS!
WELL...
SOME-TIMES. NOW, COME ON!

YAHH!
FORGET ABOUT ME?
IN TEXAS RECENTLY, A TIGER RIPPED THE ARM OFF HIS TRAINER, A FULL-GROWN MAN!
IT WOULD HAVE TAKEN MORE OF HIM IF SOMEONE HADN'T STOPPED IT!
EW!
I'M SURE YOU GIRLS LIKE YOUR LIMBS ATTACHED!
THE PLACE TO KEEP THEM THAT WAY IS IN YOUR CAR, WITH THE WINDOWS ROLLED UP!

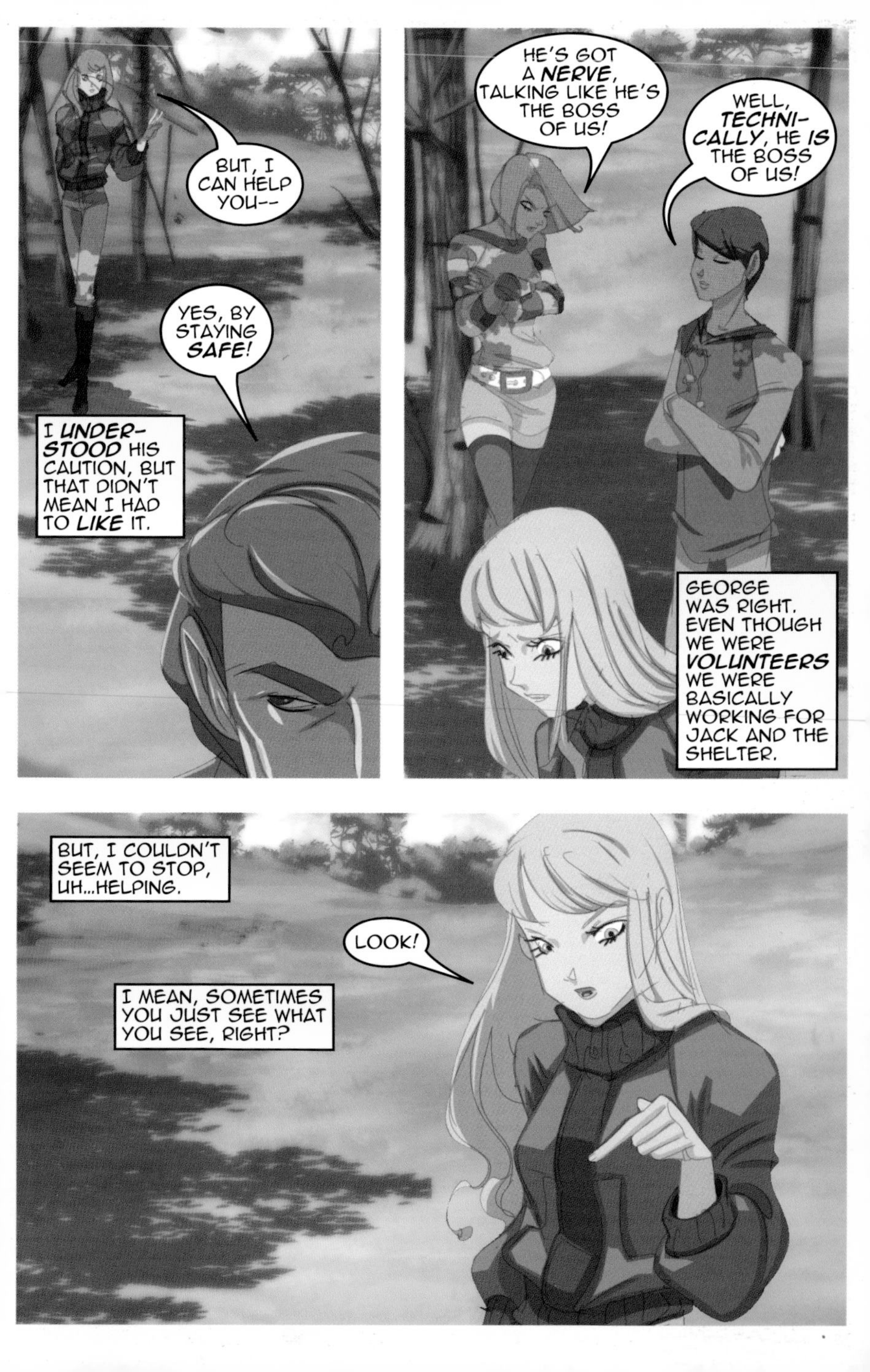
BUT, I CAN HELP YOU--
YES, BY STAYING SAFE!
I UNDER-STOOD HIS CAUTION, BUT THAT DIDN'T MEAN I HAD TO LIKE IT.
HE'S GOT A NERVE, TALKING LIKE HE'S THE BOSS OF US!
WELL, TECHNI-CALLY, HE IS THE BOSS OF US!
GEORGE WAS RIGHT. EVEN THOUGH WE WERE VOLUNTEERS WE WERE BASICALLY WORKING FOR JACK AND THE SHELTER.
BUT, I COULDN'T SEEM TO STOP, UH...HELPING.
LOOK!
I MEAN, SOMETIMES YOU JUST SEE WHAT YOU SEE, RIGHT?

A SECOND SET OF TIGER TRACKS!

YOU'RE RIGHT! THE FIRST TRACKS HEAD IN A DIFFERENT DIRECTION!

I DON'T GET IT.
DID THE TIGER COME BACK?

HMM. THESE TRACKS ARE PRETTY *DEEP*. LOOKS LIKE THERE *COULD* HAVE BEEN SEVERAL HUNDRED EXTRA POUNDS IN THAT VAN.

THE WEIGHT OF TWO *REALLY BIG* TIGERS. EEP.

BUT THE DRIVER SAID THERE WAS ONE TIGER!
YEAH, AND WHY WOULD AN ILLEGAL ANIMAL DEALER LIE?!
JACK'S ONLY LOOKING FOR ONE TIGER. SO HE'S IN FOR A SURPRISE. WE HAVE TO WARN HIM.
NO CELL PHONE SIGNAL OUT HERE.
I'LL BET JACK HASN'T GOT ONE EITHER. HE WON'T BE ABLE TO CALL FOR HELP IF HE NEEDS IT.

WHAT HAVE WE GOT HERE?
A STRETCHER, FIRST AID KIT AND THE SNARE THAT LOOKS TOO SMALL FOR ANIMALS THIS SIZE.
HEY! WE WEREN'T CRAZY ABOUT WANDERING THE WOODS WITH **ONE** TIGER LOOSE!
WHAT MAKES YOU THINK WE LIKE OUR ODDS **BETTER** WITH **TWO**?
AND WHAT'S THIS? *HMM....*
C'MON, WE HAVE TO HURRY. WE COULD BE SAVING JACK'S LIFE.
BUT **HE'S** THE ONE WITH THE **GUN**!
WHY DON'T WE JUST DRIVE TO WHERE WE CAN GET A PHONE SIGNAL AND CALL THE POLICE?

THAT MIGHT BE TOO LATE. BESIDES, CHIEF McGINNIS PROBABLY HAS HIS DEPUTIES HELPING HIM CATCH THAT DRIVER.
HE'LL HEAD BACK HERE SOON AND CATCH UP WITH US.
OH, YEAH, HE'LL BE TOTALLY THRILLED TO FIND WE DIRECTLY DISOBEYED HIM, ESPECIALLY AFTER I BROKE HIS NEW TOY!
BUT, IMAGINE HOW GRATEFUL HE'LL BE WHEN HE FINDS YOU'VE SAVED A MAN'S LIFE.
THE MAN WHO TAUGHT YOU ALL THE BEST WEB SITES FOR ANIMAL RESEARCH.
SIGH OKAY! OKAY!

BESS? COME WITH?
WAIT! WE'RE NOT GOING IN THERE ARMED WITH ONLY A FIRST AID KIT. WE NEED PRO-TECTION!
BUT THERE **AREN'T** ANY MORE TRANQUILIZER GUNS!
TOO BAD. I'D HAVE YOU USE IT ON **ME**! HUNTING TIGERS IS A NEW LEVEL OF DARING EVEN FOR **YOU**, NANCY DREW.
I HAVE JUST THE THING TO SCARE THE FUR BALLS OUT OF ANY KITTY... NO MATTER **HOW** BIG.

MACE AND AIR HORN!
NEVER LEAVE HOME WITHOUT 'EM.
YOU DO UNDERSTAND THESE ARE TIGERS... NOT CAR-JACKERS OR PURSE-SNATCHERS?

BLAAAAAAAAP!
AHHHHH!

SEE? WORKS ON *ANY-THING*!
I HATE THIS DAY.

WAIT! THE SKY'S CLOUDY! SHOULD I BRING AN *UMBRELLA* IN CASE IT RAINS?
LEAVE IT! WE'RE ALREADY CARRYING PLENTY AND WE'LL BE BACK BEFORE IT RAINS! NOW, COME ON!

LIONS AND TIGERS AND BEARS!
SIGH
OH, MY.
IT'S NO YELLOW BRICK ROAD, BUT THE JACK-TRACKS ARE DEFINITELY FOLLOWING THE FIRST SET OF TIGER-TRACKS.
I SORT OF WISHED IT WERE THE WICKED WITCH WE WERE AFTER, THEN WE COULD JUST ADD WATER.

SPEAKING OF JACK, YOU KNOW, I THINK HE MADE AN EXCELLENT POINT ABOUT LOSING LIMBS AND STAYING IN THE CAR.
THEY CALL THEM MAN-EATING TIGERS, BUT I FIGURE THEY'RE JUST AS LIKELY TO BE GIRL-EATING!
NOT HELPFUL.
NOT SO MUCH.
LOOK! MORE TRACKS OVER THERE!
WHA?
LOOK! OVER HERE, TOO! THERE ARE TRACKS ALL OVER THE PLACE!
HEY!
MY PALS HAVE BOLDLY FACED CRIMINALS OF ALL SHAPES AND EVILNESS.
SO I WAS SURPRISED TO SEE THEM SO JITTERY ABOUT ANIMALS WHO, AS FAR AS WE KNEW, HAD COMMITTED NO CRIME AT ALL!

EEP! WE'RE NOT TRACKING THEM.
THEY'RE STALKING US!
BUT, I GUESS THE WHOLE BEING EATEN-ALIVE THING JUST GETS TO SOME PEOPLE.

CALM DOWN, PLEASE! LET'S TAKE A BREATH AND A CLOSER LOOK, OKAY? I'M SURE WE'RE NOT BEING STALKED.
SEE? JACK'S TRACKS HEAD THAT WAY. THIS OTHER SET OF TIGER TRACKS CIRCLE AROUND...

KRACKLE
ULP
...RIGHT BEHIND US!
OKAY. WE WERE BEING STALKED AND WORSE, I HEARD IT COMING CLOSER.

IT'S COMING STRAIGHT FOR US.
I HEAR IT. SHOULDN'T WE CLIMB A TREE OR SOME-THING?
GREAT IDEA!
BRAKK KRKL
BUT THERE AREN'T ANY BRANCHES TO GRAB!
WE'RE DOOMED!
INCREDIBLY BAD DAY.

IT WAS TOO LATE FOR THE TREES ANYWAY.
THE THING WAS JUST A FEW FEET AWAY NOW...
BRAKK
KRKL
WHOOSH!
AND THERE IT WAS!

RUN!

WHAT DO YOU THINK I'M DOING?
DON'T PANIC!
NANCY, THIS IS NO TIME FOR A JOKE!

HEY, WAIT A MINUTE.
THAT'S NO TIGER!

IT'S A COYOTE!
WHY'D IT CHASE US?

I DON'T THINK IT WAS CHASING US.
I THINK IT WAS...

RUNNING AWAY FROM SOMETHING!

AND SOMETHING TOLD ME IT WASN'T JACK!

IT WAS A COUPLE HUNDRED POUNDS OF TIGER...
...MOVING VERY FAST!
END CHAPTER TWO

NOWHERE TO RUN...
NOWHERE TO HIDE...
UNABLE TO SCREAM...
CHAPTER THREE: PUSS IN CAHOOTS
WE HELD OUR BREATH...
AS TIME STOOD STILL.

THEN THERE WAS A SCREAM... A TERRIBLE BLAST TO THE EARS.
EVEN IF SHE THOUGHT THE IDEA WAS SILLY WHEN SHE FIRST HEARD IT, GEORGE'S GOOD REFLEXES ENABLED HER TO PUSH THE BUTTON ON THE AIR HORN...
PWWEEEE
...SCARING ME OUT OF MY CURRENT PARALYSIS.
THE PAINFUL BLAST DISTRACTED THE TIGER...
...FOR A SECOND.
RROOAR
BUT, RATHER THAN SCARING IT AWAY...

IT LOOKS LIKE YOU ONLY MADE IT *MAD*!
JUST WAIT 'TIL IT GETS TO KNOW ME!
DO YOU SEE WHAT A REALLY BAD DAY THIS IS?
GEORGE CAN BE PRETTY FUNNY WHEN SHE'S NERVOUS AND ABOUT TO DIE.

EASY, BIG FELLA! *LOOK*! NO MORE NASTY HORN.
TOO LATE TO MAKE NICE, GEORGE. TIME FOR PLAN *B*!

ROOWWLLL
PSSSSTT
BESS WAS RIGHT. IT WAS WAY TOO LATE TO MAKE NICE...

BUT IT'S **NEVER** TOO LATE TO TICK A TIGER OFF EVEN **MORE**!
CLEARLY, WE HADN'T THOUGHT THIS THROUGH.
SNARRRLLL
YEEEIII!
WE WERE RUNNING OUT OF OPTIONS, AND WE DIDN'T HAVE MANY TO BEGIN WITH!
RUN! I'LL HOLD HIM OFF.
HOW? BY LETTING HIM EAT YOU **FIRST**?

BANG
BOOOOM
GASP!
WHAT WAS THAT? IT SOUNDED LIKE A GUN SHOT!
OR THUNDER.
SOUNDED LIKE BOTH...
BUT MY MONEY'S ON THE GUN SHOT BEING WHAT SCARED OUR BIG CAT OFF.

UNLESS THERE'S ANOTHER HUNTER IN THIS FOREST, THAT GUN SHOT MEANS JACK IS CLOSE AND HE HAS THE OTHER TIGER.
OR IT HAS *HIM*!
YEAH, BUT IF THAT OTHER BOOM WAS *THUNDER*, IT'S PROBABLY GONNA...
...RAIN.
WE *COULDN'T* JUST LET BESS BRING THE *UMBRELLA*, HUH? THIS IS *SUCH* A BAD DAY.

THE STRETCHER WAS NO UMBRELLA. IT'S CANVAS WAS SOON *SOAKED* AND DRIPPING, BUT IT WAS BETTER THAN NOTHING AND A GOOD WAY FOR US TO STICK TOGETHER.
WE FOLLOWED JACK'S TRACKS UNTIL THEY ALL WERE WASHED AWAY BY THE DOWNPOUR.
SO, WE TRIED TO HEAD IN THE DIRECTION OF THE GUN SHOT SOUND, BUT IT WAS KIND OF HARD TO TELL *WHERE* THAT WAS EXACTLY.
NOW MIGHT BE A GOOD TIME TO BAG THIS BAD DAY ADVENTURE AND HEAD BACK TO THE CAR.
YEAH, ABOUT THAT.
I WAS SO BUSY LOOKING AT THE GROUND FOR TRACKS I FORGOT TO LOOK FOR *LANDMARKS*. SORRY.
SO, WE HAVE *NO IDEA* WHERE WE'RE GOING?
BASICALLY.
WE'LL STICK TO HIGH GROUND SO THAT WE DON'T GET STUCK IN A FLOODED SWAMP.
WOULDN'T *THAT* BE A FINE END TO THIS PERFECT DAY?

HELLO!
MRRROW
A FELLOW WANDERER.
ARE YOU LOST, TOO?
AGH!
GUESS IT THINKS WE'RE NOT WET **ENOUGH**. THIS HAS DEFINITELY BEEN A ***BAD DAY***.

WHERE YOU GOING?
I'M NO DETECTIVE, BUT I'D GUESS IT'S PROBABLY HEADED... THERE!
IT'S OLD LADY EARTHA'S HOUSE.
FANTASTIC! WE CAN CALL FOR HELP AND DRY OFF!

BUT, I'D BEEN A LITTLE TOO OPTIMISTIC...
COME IN?! OF COURSE, NOT! I NEVER LET STRANGERS INTO MY HOME, NEVER!
BUT WE'RE NOT STRANGERS!
WE'RE THE RESCUE VOLUNTEERS WHO CAME OUT HERE WITH JACK KINGSLEY, THE GUY WHO SAVED ONE OF YOUR CATS FROM A COYOTE...
...AND THEN TOOK MOST OF YOUR CATS AWAY. HEH!
WAIT! PLEASE. WE FOUND ONE OF YOUR CATS!

THERE'S MY LITTLE JIMINY! THOUGHT THE COYOTES GOT YOU.
PLEASE! WE'RE SOAKED AND NEED HELP, TOO.
SIGH. WELL, IF I LET YOU IN, YOU HAVE TO PROMISE NOT TO TAKE ANY MORE OF MY CATS!
WE PROMISE!
COME ON IN AND DRY YER DERRIÈRES.

I'M JUST A SUCKER FER WET STRAYS!
GASP!
FIVE!! OKAY. SO, I MAY HAVE MISSED A FEW TIGER TRACKS.

AND THAT VAN DRIVER WAS A MUCH BIGGER LIAR THAN WE THOUGHT.
AW, NOW LOOK WHAT YOU'VE DONE! JIMINY'S GOT OUT AGAIN! CLOSE THAT DOOR!
WHAT SAY WE CLOSE IT FROM THE OUTSIDE?
YEAH. THERE ARE SO MANY WORSE THINGS THAN A LITTLE RAIN. ETS-LAY O-GAY, ANCY-NAY!
ULP.
GRRRLLL

SLAM
NOW WOULD BE A PERFECT TIME TO CALL FOR HELP.
THEN, WE CAN ALL GO, PERHAPS THROUGH A KITCHEN DOOR. MRS. EARTHA, WHERE'S YOUR PHONE?
YOU'LL CALL THAT NASTY CAT-NAPPER, WON'T YOU?
HE'LL WANT TO TAKE MY NEW PETS! AND THESE LITTLE FELLAS CAN HANDLE THE COYOTES EASY!
CLEARLY THE "LITTLE FELLAS" WERE STARTING TO GET EDGY.

NOW YOU'VE UPSET THEM! AND THEY WERE ALREADY GRUMPY ABOUT HOW LITTLE *FOOD* I HAD TO FEED THEM.
UM. WHAT SAY WE DISCUSS IT *PRIVATELY* IN THE KITCHEN, MRS. EARTHA? PLEASE?
YOU MADE A *PROMISE*!
I HATED TO BREAK A PROMISE, OF COURSE. BUT, SOMETIMES IT REALLY *IS* THE RIGHT THING TO DO.
AND TECHNICALLY, WHEN SHE SAID CATS, I WAS THINKING ABOUT SOME-THING A LITTLE SMALLER.

SO, YES, MRS. EARTHA WOULD LOSE THESE CATS, PROMISE OR NO!
BUT, FIRST I HAD TO MAKE SURE SHE LIVED TO HATE US FOR IT.
AAAGH!
SLAM

SORRY, MRS. EARTHA, BUT HUNGRY TIGERS AREN'T GREAT COMPANY.
WE'RE LUCKY THEY'RE CONTAINED IN THERE, WHILE WE CALL FOR HELP AND LEAVE THROUGH...
...OR NOT.
APPARENTLY THIS HAD BEEN A HUNTER'S COTTAGE AND MRS. EARTHA HAD NEVER CHANGED IT TO MATCH THE NEW SAFETY CODES!
NO BACK DOOR! NO WINDOW! BEST OF ALL, NO PHONE!
WE'RE TRAPPED, LIKE SWAMP DEER!
OF COURSE NOT! PHONE'S BY MY BED. YOU CAN'T TALK WHILE YOU EAT, FOR HEAVEN'S SAKE.
AHHH!
WHUMP
ROARRR

GRACIOUS, WHAT WOULD MAKE THEM SO *ANGRY*?
WHUMP
LACK OF FOOD. THE DRIVER PROBABLY FIGURED HE'D LET THE *BUYER* FEED THEM. BUT THEY NEVER GOT THERE.
RROOOOARRR

WE'D BEEN IN SOME TIGHT SITUATIONS BEFORE, BUT I COULD USE MY *WITS* TO SEE A WAY OUT.
DID I MENTION WHAT A BAD DAY THIS HAS BEEN?
YES!
ROOOOARR
THIS WAS DIFFERENT. YOU CAN'T OUTSMART *HUNGER*.
CRASH
GRRLLLWLL

NANCY, WAIT! LISTEN.
IT'S QUIET.

THEY STOPPED.

BUT, WHY?

THEY'RE GONE.

THAT'S IT, **PRINCESS**, IN YOU GO WITH YOUR PALS.
IT'S JACK KINGSLEY! WE'RE SAFE, LETS **GO**!
WAIT. I NEED TO MAKE A QUICK CALL FIRST.

I KNEW YOU WERE IN CAHOOTS WITH THAT CAT STEALER!
I ASSURE YOU, MRS. EARTHA, WE'RE NOT.
WE'RE NOT? ISN'T HE THE BOSS OF US ANYMORE?

NO. I'LL EXPLAIN WHEN CHIEF McGINNIS GETS HERE.
HELLO, THIS IS NANCY DREW. PATCH ME THROUGH TO THE CHIEF, PLEASE.

JACK! VAN DRIVER GAVE ME QUITE A RUN, BUT WE FINALLY GOT HIM!
NANCY TOLD ME YOU GOT THE TIGERS... FIVE OF 'EM!
UH, YES. I TRACKED THEM **HERE**. SEEMS THEY MADE A FRIEND OF MRS. EARTHA.
IF ***YOU*** HADN'T COME THEY WOULD HAVE MADE A MEAL OF MRS. EARTHA ***AND*** THE REST OF US!
YOU REALLY SAVED THE TOTALLY BAD DAY.
DON'T BE ***SO*** GRATEFUL, LADIES. MR. KINGSLEY WAS ALSO THE ***CAUSE*** OF THE TOTALLY BAD DAY!
JACK ***ORDERED*** THOSE TIGERS.
I WAS SUSPICIOUS ABOUT THOSE BIG CAGES HE KEPT HANDY. HIS EXPLANATION THAT THEY WERE FOR THE CAPTURE OF ILLEGAL BIG CATS WAS A LITTLE ***FLIMSY***!

YOU CAN PROBABLY CONFIRM THIS, CHIEF, BUT THERE'VE BEEN NO SUCH BIG CAT SEIZURES IN RIVER HEIGHTS...
AT LEAST NOT IN MY TIME. I READ THE PAPER EVERY DAY AND, LETS FACE IT, THAT'S BIG NEWS!
NOW THAT YOU MENTION IT, I CAN'T RECALL ANY IN MY TIME ON THE FORCE.
THEN IN THE FIRST AID KIT, I FOUND THIS FAX WITH A LIST OF NAMES AND VACCINE REQUIRE-MENTS.
ACCORDING TO THE DATE IT WAS SENT TO JACK YESTER-DAY.
IT WAS WITH THIS BOTTLE OF FEL-O-VAX A BIG CAT VACCINE WHICH ISN'T USUALLY KEPT IN AN EMERGENCY FIRST AID KIT!
Fel-O-Vax
I WOULD HAVE ASKED YOU ABOUT IT, BUT YOU GAVE YOURSELF AWAY WHEN YOU WERE PUTTING THE TIGERS IN THE VAN AND CALLED ONE PRINCESS. THAT'S A NAME ON THIS LIST.
YOU WERE CONDUCTING YOUR OWN ILLEGAL TIGER SALES, WEREN'T YOU?
princesss
THIS WAS THE BIGGEST ORDER I'D EVER PROCESSED, AND I ADMIT I WENT TOO FAR.
BUT THEY WOULD ALL HAVE GOTTEN GOOD HOMES.

I'M SURE YOU WANTED THE BEST FOR THE CATS, JACK, AND FOR YOURSELF! BUT, IT'S STILL ILLEGAL!
AND THEN THERE'S THE LITTLE MATTER OF ENDANGERING THE LIVES OF OUR FINE CITIZENS.
SO, ANOTHER ADVENTURE WITHOUT A SCRATCH!
YOU GIRLS ARE LIKE CATS, BUT YOU SEEM TO HAVE A LOT MORE THAN NINE LIVES.
OH, AND THEY WERE ABLE TO FIX MY NEW MDT, GEORGE!
GREAT! CAN I TRY IT WHILE YOU DRIVE US BACK?
NOT ON YOUR LIFE! YOU CAN RIDE WITH THE TIGERS... IF YOU DON'T MIND THE SMELL.
COUGH THIS HAS DEFINITELY BEEN...
WE KNOW, A BAD DAY.
THE END

NANCY DREW, GIRL DETECTIVE, HERE TO TELL YOU THAT NO MATTER WHAT YOUR FRIENDS MAY SAY, SOMETIMES BEING FULL OF HOT AIR IS A *GOOD THING*.
LIKE DURING THE *RIVER HEIGHTS ANNUAL BALLOON EXPO*, FOR INSTANCE.
BALLOONING IS A SPORT THAT TAKES A *LOT* OF HOT AIR.
CHAPTER ONE:
WHAT GOES UP...

SOMEONE EXPLAIN HOW THESE THINGS WORK. **QUICK**.
BALLOONS CARRYING PEOPLE FEELS LIKE SOMETHING THAT SHOULD ONLY HAPPEN IN ***CARTOONS***!
OKEY DOKE! HOT AIR BALLOONS ARE BASED ON A VERY FUNDAMENTAL SCIENTIFIC PRINCIPLE... WARMER AIR ***RISES*** IN COOLER AIR!
UH-OH. HERE WE GO...
ESSEN-TIALLY, HOT AIR IS LIGHTER THAN COOL AIR, BECAUSE IT HAS LESS MASS PER UNIT OF VOLUME.
A CUBIC FOOT OF AIR WEIGHS ROUGHLY 28 GRAMS.
I'M SO ***BORED*** I'M NOT SCARED ANYMORE. THANKS, NANCY.
IF YOU HEAT THAT AIR BY 100 DEGREES FAHRENHEIT, IT WEIGHS ABOUT 7 GRAMS LESS.

SO EACH CUBIC FOOT OF AIR INSIDE THE BALLOON CAN LIFT ABOUT 7 GRAMS.
NOW, THAT'S NOT MUCH, WHICH IS WHY THESE SUCKERS ARE SO HUMUNGOUS!
WHY, TO LIFT 1,000 POUNDS, YOU'D NEED ABOUT 65,000 CUBIC FEET OF HOT AIR!
NANCY, PLEASE...
I SWEAR I'LL NEVER BE AFRAID AGAIN. JUST PLEASE, STOP! WE'RE HERE TO HAVE FUN, NOT STUDY PHYSICS!
BUT, PHYSICS IS FUN!

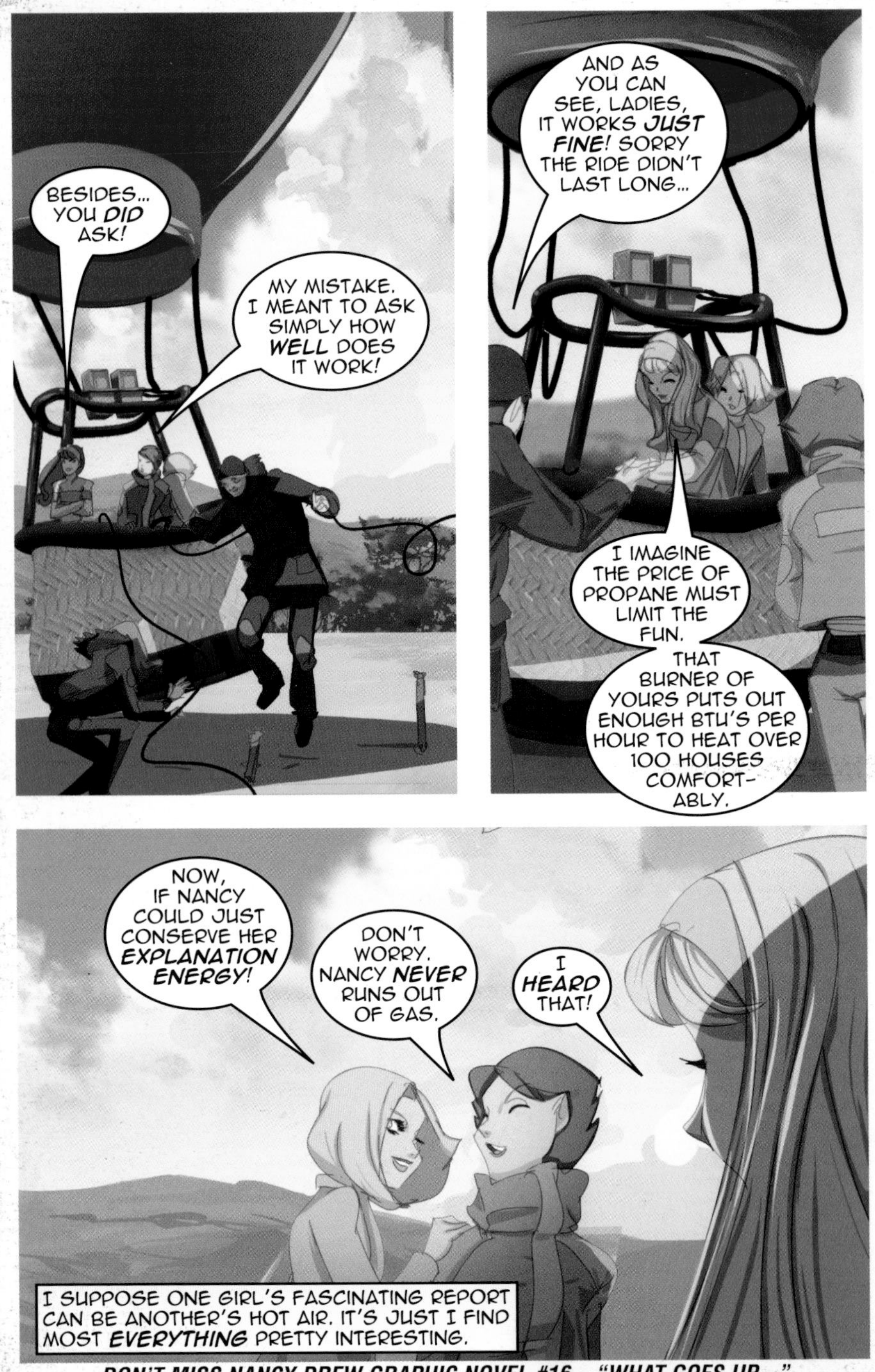

DON'T MISS NANCY DREW GRAPHIC NOVEL #16 – "WHAT GOES UP..."

WATCH OUT FOR PAPERCUTZ™

Guess what? If you're reading this, that means you may be a Papercutz person. Don't panic -- that's a good thing. It means you're not only enjoying the latest, greatest Nancy Drew graphic novel, but you're part of a special club that's on the cutting edge of pop culture entertainment.

Let's back up a little. If you're just joining the Papercutz party, allow me to indroduce myself. I'm Jim Salicrup, Papercutz Editor-in-Chief. It's my happy responsibility to produce the best graphic novels for people of all ages. Graphic novels, as I'm sure you're hip enough to know, are simply comicbooks disguised as regular books. Or as some people say "real books."

Graphic novels also happen to be the latest thing to take the publishing world by storm. Just a few years ago, only comic-book publishers produced graphic novels, but now just about every big-time publisher there is wants to get in on the act. And you know, we think that's terrific. The more publishers giving opportunities to writers and artists to create all-new graphic novels, the greater the chances are that we'll get to see some amazing new graphic novels from new writers and artists.

On the other hand, with so many graphic novels being produced at such a rapid rate -- more now than ever before -- it's easy to be completely overwhelmed by it all. How can anyone know which graphic novels to choose, with so many to pick from? Well, we have one helpful suggestion. If you like the graphic novel you're reading now, chances are you may enjoy other Papercutz graphic novels. In the following pages, you'll find some sample pages from TALES FROM THE CRYPT, which features several scary stories within each volume.

So, check us out. If you like what you see, you may just be a Papercutz person. And, as we said, that's a good thing.

Thanks,

Caricature by Rick Parker

-Greetings, Fiends!

It's your ol' pal the CRYPT-KEEPER here, giving a guided TERRIFYING TOUR through the SCARIEST GRAPHIC NOVEL ever! It's TALES FROM THE CRYPT #4 "CRYPT-KEEPING IT REAL."

You'll not only find page after page of PULSE-POUNDING CHILLS, but me and my fellow GhouLunatics decided to get all COMPUTER AGE-Y on you! Wait till you see the stories we found on the INTERRED-NET site known as YOU-TOOMB! The SHOCKS and SUSPENSE come at you FAST and FURIOUS!

But that's not all! Just gaze upon the CREEPY COVER on the next page, if you DARE! That poor guy made the UNFORTUNATE MISTAKE of appearing on a REALITY TV SHOW that was perhaps a little TOO REAL! The show is called "JUMPING THE SHARK" and you can see a quick preview starting right after the next PUTRID PAGE!

ALL-NEW STORIES! FULL-COLOR GRAPHIC NOVEL!
TERROR
TALES FROM THE CRYPT
NO. 4
CRYPT-KEEPING IT REAL
AN ENTERTAINING EC COMIC
FEATURING 2 ALL-NEW STORIES BY
JOE R. LANSDALE &
JOHN L. LANSDALE
TODAY'S TOP HORROR WRITERS!
FEATURING...
THE CRYPT-KEEPER
THE OLD WITCH
THE VAULT-KEEPER
PAPERCUTZ

WELCOME BACK TO "JUMPING THE SHARK!" WHEN WE LAST LEFT YOU, CAITLIN WAS ABOUT TO EAT THIS JAR OF MAGGOTS...
EAT THE MAGGOTS! EAT THE MAGGOTS! EAT THE MAGGOTS!
SHE DID IT!!
GULP!
EEEEWWWW!
THE MAN WITH THE DARK SHADES IS PRODUCER LAZLO SLOAN. "JUMPING THE SHARK" IS HIS BABY.
PHIL, YOU IDIOT! THE NEXT TIME YOU'RE THIS LATE WITH MY COFFEE, YOU'RE FIRED!!
SORRY, MR. SLOAN, SIR!
THE MAN WALKING AWAY... WELL, THAT'S ME. I'M PHIL RAFFERTY, LAZLO'S ASSISTANT.
SOME DAY THAT STUPID OLD COOT'S GOING TO GET HIS!

A COUPLE OF COMMERCIAL BREAKS LATER...
WHEN WE LAST LEFT YOU, RANDY HAD MADE IT UP TO THE FINAL LEVEL ON THE SHOW--*THE SHARK-INFESTED TANK!*
SNAP!
SPLOOSH!

HEY! COME ON, PEOPLE! THIS IS NO BIG DEAL! PLEASE STAY IN YOUR SEATS!
...UH...
THIS CAN'T BE HAPPEN- ING!
THE VERY NEXT DAY...
WHAT HAPPENED TO RANDY EVANS WAS A TRAGEDY. BUT I THINK WE CAN ALL AGREE THAT HE KNEW WHAT HE WAS GETTING HIMSELF INTO. NO ONE PUT A GUN TO HIS HEAD AND SAID, "HEY YOU, SIGN THIS WAIVER!"
BUT MR. SLOAN--
NO MORE QUESTIONS!
GO TO RANDY'S FAMILY. WRITE THEM A CHECK-- LET THEM NAME THE AMOUNT...
MR. SLOAN-- THAT'S IMMORAL!
IMMORAL? WHAT IS THIS, KINDERGARTEN?! JUST SHUT UP AND GET THEM TO TAKE THE MONEY!!
THAT WAS THE LAST STRAW. SOMEONE HAD TO TEACH HIM A LESSON...

What happens next will SHOCK you, as you'll find out in
TALES FROM THE CRYPT Graphic Novel #4 "Crypt-Keeping It Real"!

THE HARDY BOYS

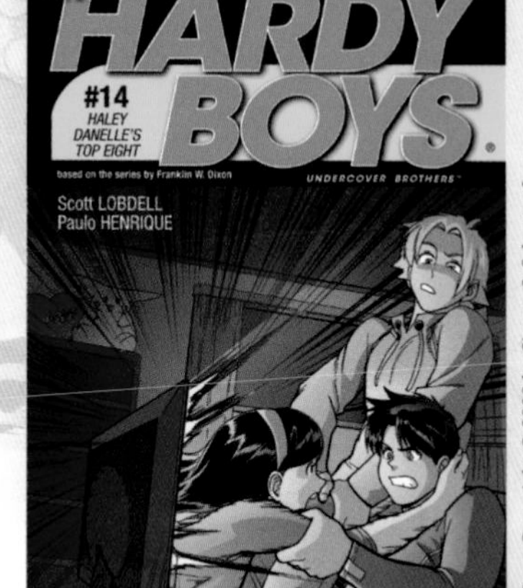

A NEW GRAPHIC NOVEL EVERY 3 MONTHS!

#10 "A Hardy Day's Night"
ISBN - 978-1-59707-070-6
#11 "Abracadeath"
ISBN - 978-1-59707-080-5
#12 "Dude Ranch O' Death"
ISBN - 978-1-59707-088-1
#13 "The Deadliest Stunt"
ISBN - 978-1-59707-102-4
NEW! #14 "Haley Danielle's Top Eight!"
ISBN – 978-159707-113-0
Also available – Hardy Boys #1-9
All: Pocket sized, 96-112 pp., full-color, $7.95
Also available in hardcover! $12.95

THE HARDY BOYS
Graphic Novels #1-4 Box Set
ISBN – 978-1-59707-040-9
THE HARDY BOYS
Graphic Novels #5-8 Box Set
ISBN – 978-1-59707-075-1
THE HARDY BOYS
Graphic Novels #9-12 Box Set
ISBN-978-1-59707-125-3
All: Full-color, $29.95

#1 "Great Expectations"
ISBN 978-159707-097-3
#2 "The Invisible Man"
ISBN 978-159707-106-2
NEW! #3 "Through the Looking Glass"
ISBN 978-159707-115-4
All: 6 1/2 x 9, 56 pp., full-color, $9.95

Please add $4.00 postage and handling. Make check payable to NBM publishing.
Send To:
Papercutz, 40 Exchange Place, Suite 1308,
New York, New York 10005, 1-800-886-1223
www.papercutz.com